PRESENTED TO

John Edward Patrick Sutton

ON THE OCCASION OF

his Confirmation

BY

Grandma and Grandad

ON

July 12th 2022

GIFTS OF THE HOLY SPIRIT

ANOINTED

Written by **Pope Francis**

Compiled and edited by
Jaymie Stuart Wolfe

Pauline
BOOKS & MEDIA
Boston

ISBN 10: 0–8198–0653–6

ISBN 13: 978–0-8198–0653–6

Adapted by the Daughters of St. Paul

Biography of Pope Francis by Mary Lea Hill, FSP

Cover and interior design by Putri Mamesah (novice, Daughters of St. Paul) and Mary Joseph Peterson, FSP

Published by Pauline Books & Media, 50 Saint Pauls Avenue, Boston, MA 02130–3491

Printed in Korea

www.pauline.org

Pauline Books & Media is the publishing house of the Daughters of St. Paul, an international congregation of women religious serving the Church with the communications media.

1 2 3 4 5 6 7 8 9   21 20 19 18 17

CONTENTS

FOREWORD

After Jesus ascended to heaven, his original disciples and the Blessed Virgin Mary gathered in the Upper Room. There, they waited for the Holy Spirit to come as Jesus had promised. Like you, they may have wondered if the Spirit really would come, or what difference it could make in their lives. A few days later, they learned the truth. God kept his promise (he always does!), and the Holy Spirit changed everything. Cowards became courageous, simple people became wise and knowledgeable, prayer became dynamic, and the mission of bringing the Good News of salvation in Christ took off like a rocket. We celebrate that amazing event every Pentecost. But we also know that God wants to give each and every one of us a *personal* Pentecost. That is what Confirmation is meant to be.

You have been—or are about to be—Confirmed. When you receive the sacrament of Confirmation, you will be more than just a full-fledged Catholic. You will be anointed with the oil of Chrism, and with a fresh outpouring of God's Holy Spirit. That's something to be excited about! Why? Because living our faith isn't something we can do on our own. Every one of us is dependent on the power and presence of the Holy Spirit. And that is God's gift to us at Confirmation.

God, however, never gets tired of giving us gifts. But the fact that God gives us something, doesn't mean we actually receive it. This book is intended to help you unwrap, open, and receive all the gifts that God has already given you to enjoy and share.

In 2014, our Holy Father Pope Francis gave a series of talks about the gifts of the Holy Spirit at his weekly "Wednesday Audiences" in Rome. The words in this book are selected from those teachings. As the editor of *Anointed*, I have chosen words I believe will inspire and encourage you. They are accompanied by vibrant images and color to help you encounter what Pope Francis has to say to you in an easy-to-read way.

May this book help you to experience God's great love for you, and learn to trust that the Holy Spirit will empower and assist you every day of your life. All God's gifts are yours. You are his anointed.

Jaymie Stuart Wolfe, Editor

INTRODUCTION BY POPE FRANCIS

The Holy Spirit is the soul, the lifeblood of the Church and of every individual Christian. He is the Love of God who makes his dwelling place in our hearts and enters into communion with us. The Holy Spirit abides with us, and stays with us, always. He is always within us, in our hearts.

The Spirit himself is the most excellent "gift of God," and he in turn communicates various spiritual gifts to those who receive him. The Church identifies *seven gifts*, a number which symbolizes *fullness* and *completeness*. These are the gifts we learn about when we prepare for the sacrament of Confirmation. They are also the gifts we ask for at Pentecost in the ancient prayer that is called the Sequence of the Holy Spirit. The gifts of the Holy Spirit are *wisdom, understanding, counsel, fortitude, knowledge, piety,* and the *fear of the Lord.*

WISDOM

From the Teaching of Pope Francis—April 9, 2014

The first gift
of the Holy Spirit
is wisdom.

But it is not simply human wisdom, which is the fruit of knowledge and experience. . . . Wisdom is the grace of being able *to see everything with the eyes of God*. . . . It is to see the world; to see situations, circumstances, problems, everything through God's eyes.

Sometimes we see things according to our own likes and dislikes, or perhaps with love or hate or envy or whatever is in our own hearts. . . . But this is not *God's* perspective.

Wisdom is the Holy Spirit's work in us. The gift of wisdom enables us to see things with the eyes of God.

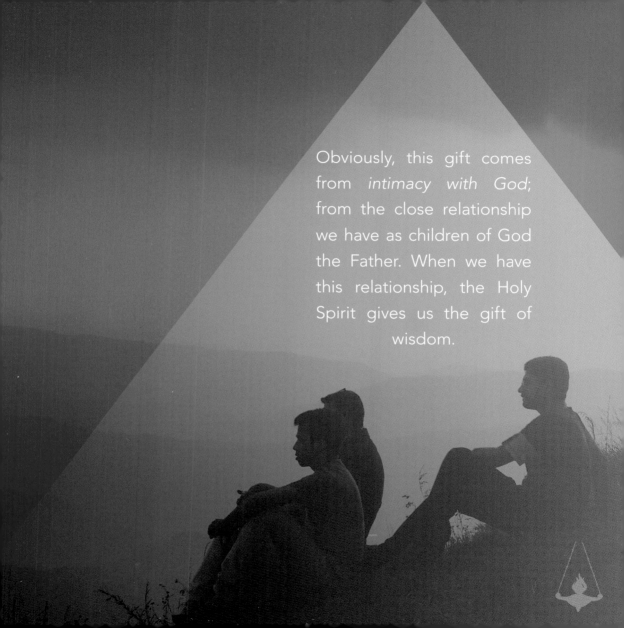

Obviously, this gift comes from *intimacy with God*; from the close relationship we have as children of God the Father. When we have this relationship, the Holy Spirit gives us the gift of wisdom.

The Holy Spirit . . . makes the Christian "wise." Not in the sense that we have answers for everything, but in the sense that we "*know*" *God.* We know how God acts, when something is of God and when it is not of God, because we have the wisdom God places in our hearts.

The heart of a wise person

has a *taste* for God and savors him. And how important it is that there are Christians like this in our communities! Everything in them speaks of God and becomes a beautiful and living sign of his presence and his love.

This is the wisdom the Holy Spirit gives freely to us, and we can all have it. . . . We only have to ask the Holy Spirit for it. Wisdom cannot be learned; it is a gift of the Holy Spirit. Therefore, we must ask the Lord to fill us with the Holy Spirit and to give us the gift of wisdom. The wisdom of God teaches us to see with God's eyes, to feel with God's heart, and to speak with God's words.

Choose my teaching
rather than silver,
And knowledge
instead of pure gold;
for wisdom
is more valuable than jewels,
and all you desire
can't compare with her.

See Proverbs 8:10-11

Come, Spirit of Wisdom.

Show me the power and beauty of heavenly things.
Teach me to love them more than all the passing joys
and satisfactions of this earth. Grant that I may always
put the things of God first in my life until the day when
I am united with you forever in heaven. Amen.

UNDERSTANDING

From the Teaching of Pope Francis—April 30, 2014

We are not dealing here with human understanding, or with our different abilities to think and learn. The gift of understanding is a grace which only the Holy Spirit can pour into us. For a Christian, this gift awakens an ability to go beyond the outward appearance of reality and to probe the depth of God's thoughts and his plan of salvation.

This does not mean that a Christian can comprehend all things and have complete knowledge of God's designs. . . .
But the effect of this gift is that we can understand a situation in depth, as God understands it.

to probe the depths
of God's thoughts
and his plan of
salvation.

obe the depths
od's thoughts
is plan of

Jesus wanted to send us the Holy Spirit so that we all might understand things the way God does, to understand things with the mind of God. What a beautiful gift the Lord has given us! With this gift the Holy Spirit brings us close to God and makes us sharers in the plan of love which he has for us.

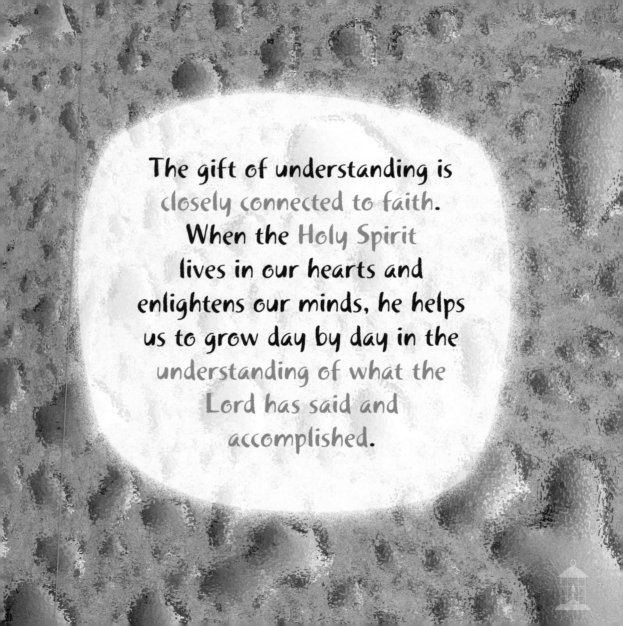

The gift of understanding is
closely connected to faith.
When the Holy Spirit
lives in our hearts and
enlightens our minds, he helps
us to grow day by day in the
understanding of what the
Lord has said and
accomplished.

understanding

Jesus told his disciples: I will send you the Holy Spirit and he will enable you to understand all that I have taught you. With the help of the Holy Spirit, we can understand the teachings of Jesus, understand the Gospel, and understand the Word of God.

understanding

Anyone can read the Gospel and understand something. But if we read the Gospel with this gift of the Holy Spirit, we can understand the depth of God's words.

understanding

After witnessing the death of Jesus, two of his disciples leave Jerusalem and return to their village, Emmaus. Jesus walks with them, but they are so sad, in such deep despair, that they do not recognize him. When, however, the Lord explains the Scriptures to them, *their minds are opened and hope is rekindled in their hearts.*

See Lk 24:13–27

. . .This is what the Holy Spirit does with us: he opens our minds; **he opens us** so that we can better understand the **things of God,** human things, situations **—all things.**

I run the way of your commandments, for you enlarge my understanding.

Lord, teach me your way,
and I will observe it to the end.
Give me understanding, so I may keep your law
and obey it with my whole heart.

See Psalm 119:33–34

Prayer

Come, Spirit of Understanding.
Enlighten my mind
so that I may see more deeply into the truths
I already believe by faith.
Bring me one day
into the eternal light of your glory.
And, Holy Spirit,
give me a clear vision of you
and the Father
and the Son.
Amen.

COUNSEL

From the Teaching of Pope Francis—May 7, 2014

We know how important it is . . . to count on the advice of people who are wise and who love us.

Now, through the gift of

counsel,

God himself enlightens our hearts. He does this so that we are able to grasp the right way to speak and to behave, as well as the way to follow him.

When we receive and welcome him into our hearts,

the Holy Spirit immediately begins to guide our thoughts and make us sensitive to his voice. He shapes our feelings and our intentions according to the heart of God.

With the gift of counsel,
the Holy Spirit
makes us grow—
positively and in community with others.
The gift of counsel helps us not to fall prey to
self-centeredness and our own way of seeing things.

In closeness with God and in listening to his Word, we put aside our own way of thinking. Little by little, we open what has been closed, and let go of our prejudices and ambitions. We learn instead to ask the Lord: what is your desire? What is your will? What pleases you?

Prayer is essential if we are to hold on to this gift.

Prayer! Never forget prayer. Never! No one, no one notices when we pray on the bus or walking along the road; we can pray in the silence of our own hearts.

The Holy Spirit will counsel us about what we all must do. But we have to make room for the Spirit . . .

And to give space is to pray, to ask that he come and help us, always.

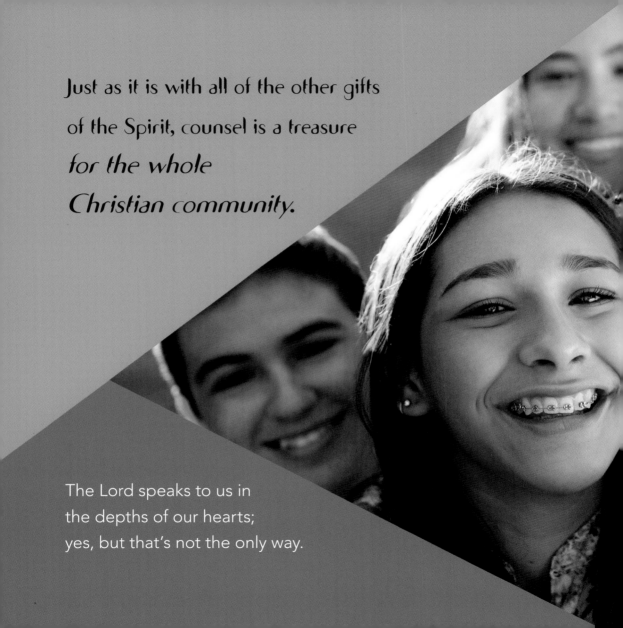

Just as it is with all of the other gifts of the Spirit, counsel is a treasure *for the whole Christian community.*

The Lord speaks to us in the depths of our hearts; yes, but that's not the only way.

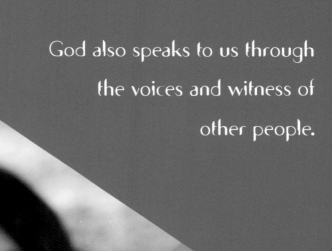

God also speaks to us through the voices and witness of other people.

It is truly a great gift to be able to meet men and women of faith who bring light to our hearts and help us to recognize the Lord's will—especially in the most complicated and important stages of our lives!

I praise the LORD; he gives me counsel.

My heart teaches me in the darkness.

I keep the Lord in my thoughts.

Because he is beside me

I shall not be moved.

See Psalm 16:7–8

COME, SPIRIT OF COUNSEL.

Help me in all my ways. Guide me, so that I may always choose what is right, even in difficult circumstances. Direct my heart to all that is good, and lead me along the path of your commandments until I reach eternal life.

Amen.

FORTITUDE

From the Teaching of Pope Francis—May 14, 2014

One day
a farmer
went out
sowing...

There is a parable *Jesus told that helps us to grasp the importance of fortitude, or strength. A sower plants seeds in the ground; however, not all of the seed which he sows bears fruit.*

. . . Only what falls
on good soil
is able to grow.

Through the gift of fortitude, the Holy Spirit liberates the soil of our heart. *He frees it from all the fears that can hinder it, so that the Lord's Word may be genuinely and joyfully put into practice.*

Sometimes we may be tempted to give in to laziness—or worse, to discouragement. This happens to us especially when we face life's hardships and trials.

When that happens, let us not lose heart. Let us call on the Holy Spirit instead. Through his gift of fortitude the Holy Spirit can lift our hearts.

He will communicate a new strength and enthusiasm to our lives and to the way we follow Jesus.

There are . . . difficult moments *and* extreme situations *in which the gift of strength and fortitude shows itself in an extraordinary way.*

The Church shines with the testimony of so many brothers and sisters who did not hesitate to sacrifice their own lives *in order to remain faithful to the Lord and his Gospel.*

Among our brothers and sisters is another kind of saint—everyday saints who are hidden saints among us. The gift of fortitude is what empowers them to carry out their responsibilities as individuals—fathers, mothers, brothers, sisters, citizens.

need to be strong every
of our lives in order to
y our lives, our families,
our faith forward. The
stle Paul said something
is good for us to hear. . . .
en we face the struggles of
y life, when difficulties
e, let us remember this:

"I can do all things **in Christ;** he strengthens me."
See Phil 4:13

The Lord always strengthens us. He never allows us to lack the strength we need. The Lord does not test us beyond our abilities. He is always with us.

I love you Lord, *my strength.*

The Lord is my rock, my fortress, and my savior,

my God, my rock in whom
I find safety,
my shield, and my salvation,
my stronghold.

I call upon the Lord.
He is worthy to be praised.
The LORD shall save me from my enemies.

See Psalm 18:1–3

Come,
Spirit of Strength.

Sustain me in times of trouble;

strengthen me in times of weakness;

give me courage in times of hardship.

Guide me as I try to live a holy life,

until the day that I join

the saints in heaven

to praise you for all eternity.

Amen.

KNOWLEDGE KNOWLEDGE K

KNOWLEDGEKNOW

From the Teaching of Pope Francis—May 21, 2014

PACITY TO LEARN AND TO DISCOVER THE LAWS OF NATURE AND

SPIRIT, HOWEVER, IS NOT LIMITED TO WHAT HUMAN BEINGS CA...

EATNESS AND LOVE AND HIS DEEP RELATIONSHIP WITH EVERY CREATURE

IN THE BEAUTY OF NATURE AND IN THE GREATNESS OF THE

G SPEAKS TO US ABOUT GOD AND HIS LOVE.

ECIATE SOMETHING MARVELOUS. THE SPIRIT INSPIRES US TO PRAIS...

LESS GIFT OF GOD AND SEE IT AS SIGN OF HIS INFINITE LOVE FOR US.

GOD IS PLEASED WITH HIS CREATION. IF GOD SEES...

HE SAME ATTITUDE AND SEE THAT CREATION IS A GOOD AND BEAUTIFUL...

E PRAISE GOD AND GIVE THANKS TO HIM FOR HAVING...

ASTERS OF CREATION. IT ALSO HELPS US TO RESIST THE TEMPTATIO...

PECTATIONS AND NEEDS. WITH THE GIFT OF KNOWLEDGE, THE SPIRIT HEL...

H THE CREATOR AND ALLOWS US TO PARTICIPAT...

When we speak of knowledge,

we immediately think of the human capacity to learn and to discover the laws of nature and the universe.

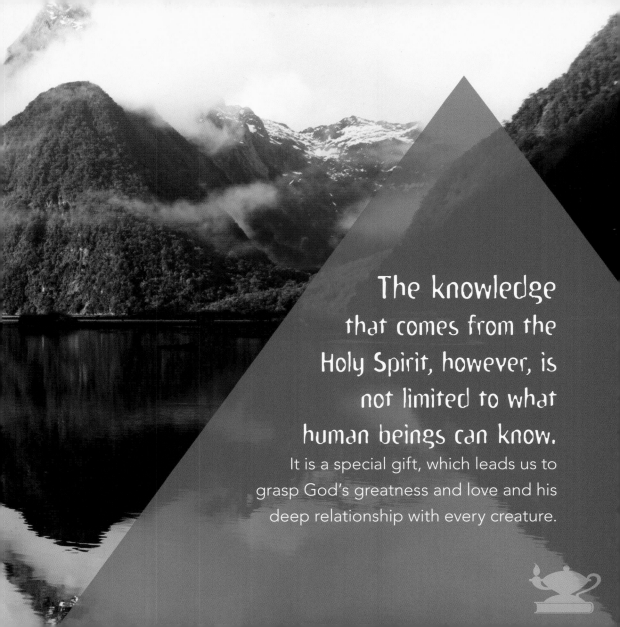

The knowledge that comes from the Holy Spirit, however, is not limited to what human beings can know. It is a special gift, which leads us to grasp God's greatness and love and his deep relationship with every creature.

When our eyes are illumined by the Spirit,

they open to see God in the beauty of nature and in the greatness of the cosmos. The Spirit leads us *to discover how everything speaks to us about God and his love.*

This is what we experience when we admire a work of art or appreciate something marvelous.

The Spirit
inspires us

to praise the Lord from the depths
of our hearts when we recognize a
priceless gift of God and see it as
a sign of his infinite love for us.

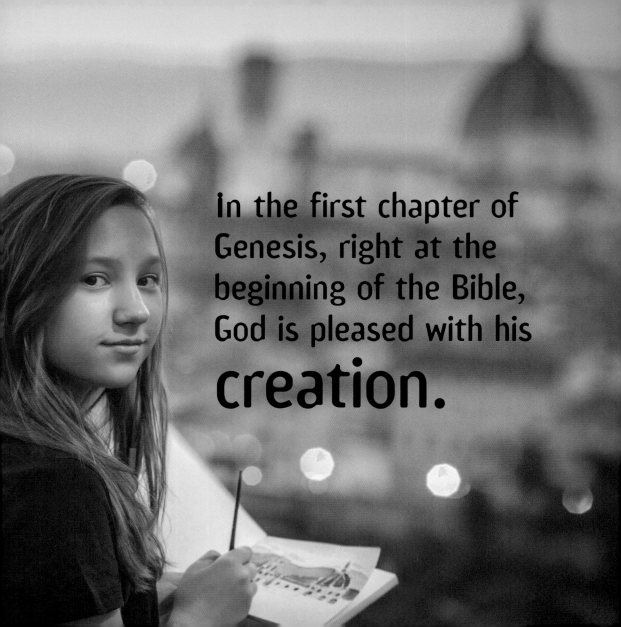

In the first chapter of Genesis, right at the beginning of the Bible, God is pleased with his **creation.**

If God sees creation as good, as a beautiful thing, then we, too, should have the same attitude and see that creation is good and beautiful.

Now, the gift of knowledge is what allows us to see this beauty. We praise God and give thanks to him for having given so much beauty to us.

THE GIFT OF KNOWLEDGE

keeps us from considering ourselves the masters of creation.

It also helps us to resist the temptation to look to creatures instead of the Creator to answer all our expectations and needs. With the gift of knowledge, the Spirit helps us not to fall into these errors.

The gift of knowledge

brings us into

harmony with the Creator

and allows us to

participate in his vision

and his judgment.

O Lord, *you have searched me and known me.*
You know when I sit and when I rise;
you perceive my thoughts from afar.
You search out my path and are familiar with all my ways.
Even before a word is on my tongue,
O Lord, *you know what I will say.*
Your presence surrounds me, behind and before me. You lay your hand upon me.
Such knowledge is too much for me;
it is so high that I cannot attain it.
How great are your thoughts, O God!
How vast is the sum of them!
If I try to count them, I cannot.
For they are more than all the grains of sand.

See Psalm 139:1-6;17-18a

Come, Spirit of Knowledge.

Give me the grace to see the things of this earth as a means to serve God and my neighbor. Show me how to glorify God in every circumstance of my life and to cherish friendship with God beyond all else. Teach me to hope in the eternal reward you promise to those who are faithful. Amen.

PIETY

From the Teaching of Pope Francis—June 4, 2014

bond

Piety is not the same as pity. . . .
The gift of piety is a sign that

we belong to God

and are deeply bonded to
him. This bond gives
meaning to every aspect
of our lives. It keeps us
firm in our communion
with God, especially in the
most difficult moments.

Our relationship with
the Lord is

. . . *lived with the heart.*

It is a friendship with God granted
to us by Jesus, a friendship that
changes our lives and fills us with
passion and joy. Thus, above all,
the gift of piety stirs gratitude and
praise in us.

celebrate

When the Holy Spirit allows us to sense
the presence of the Lord and all his love for us,

our hearts are warmed,

and we are moved
—quite naturally—
to prayer
and
celebration.

Piety, therefore, is the same as
. . . the ability to pray to God with the kind of

*love and
simplicity*

that belong to those who have humble hearts.

Some think that
to be pious is
to close one's eyes,
pose like a picture,
and pretend to be a saint.

This is not the gift of piety.

. . . Piety makes us grow in our relation and communion with God, and leads us to live as his children.

At the same time, it helps us to pour this love out to others and to recognize them as brothers and sisters.

piety

Let us ask the Lord
for the gift of piety
to conquer our fear,
our uncertainty,
and our restless,
impatient spirit.

May his Spirit make of us joyful witnesses of God and of his love,
witnesses who worship the Lord in truth
and in gentle service to our neighbor.
And, may we always have the smile
that the Holy Spirit gives us in joy.

Come!

let's sing to the Lord;

let's make a joyful noise
to the rock of our salvation!

Let's come into his presence giving thanks. . .

Come!

let's worship and bow down,

let's fall to our knees before
the Lord, our Maker!

He is our God,
and we are the people
of his pasture.
We are the sheep
of his hand.

See Psalm 95:1–2; 6–7

Come,
Spirit of Piety.

Enkindle in my heart
a love for God and my neighbor.
Inspire within me
a deep respect for others
that leads to real concern,
compassion, and care for all those in need.
Grant that in serving others
I may serve you.

Amen.

FEAR OF THE LORD

From the Teaching of Pope Francis—June 11, 2014

Fear of the Lord does not mean that we should be afraid of God. For we know that God is our Father; that he loves us and wants our salvation, and he always forgives us—always. There is no reason to be scared of God!

Through this gift we are reminded of how small we are before God. But we also remember his love for us. We know that what is best for us lies in humbly and respectfully entrusting our whole selves to his hands. This is the fear of the Lord: complete trust in the goodness of our Father who loves us so much.

This is what the Holy Spirit does in our hearts: he makes us feel like children in the arms of our father.

Fear of the Lord

makes us aware that everything comes from grace. It teaches us that our true strength is found only in following the Lord Jesus and in allowing God the Father to shower us with

his goodness and his mercy.

Fear of the Lord does not make us shy and submissive! It stirs up courage and strength in us!

It is a gift that makes us convinced and enthusiastic Christians, who obey the Lord not because we fear him, but because we are motivated and conquered by his love!

FEAR OF THE LORD

It is a beautiful thing to be

conquered by the

love of God;

to allow ourselves to be conquered by the love of a Father, who... loves us with all his heart!

Through the gift of fear of the Lord,
the Holy Spirit opens our hearts. And
our hearts must be open so that
forgiveness, mercy, goodness, and the loving
touch of the Father may come to us. We are children
infinitely loved.

I sought out the Lord, and he answered me.
He saved me from all of my fears.
Look to him, and shine;
so your faces will never be filled with shame.
When poor souls cry out, the Lord hears,
and delivers them from every trouble.

The angel of the Lord encamps around those
who fear him, and saves them.
Taste and see that the Lord is good;
those who find refuge in him are happy.
Fear the Lord, all you holy ones,
for those who fear him will have all they need.

See Psalm 34:4–9

COME, SPIRIT OF HOLY FEAR.

Fill my heart with wonder and awe of you. Creator of all that is good, true, and beautiful—give me an outpouring of your grace. Help me to see your handiwork in the beauty of creation around me, and rejoice in the presence of your splendor and majesty. Amen.

PRAYERS

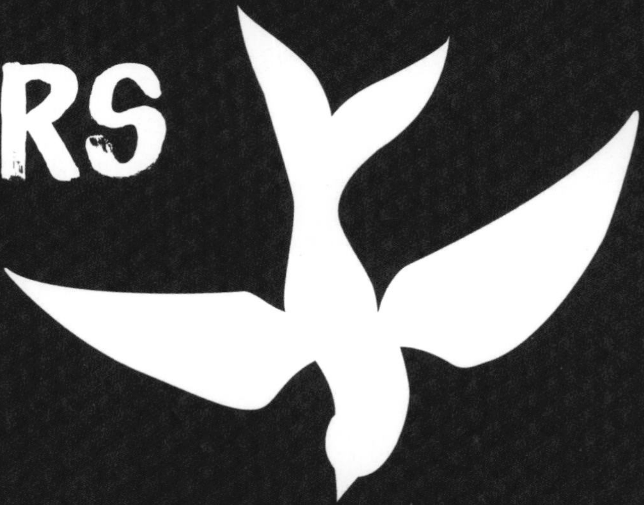

The Spirit helps us in our weakness. For though we do not know how to pray, the Holy Spirit intercedes for us with sighs deeper than words. And God, who searches the heart, knows the mind of the Spirit, because the Spirit prays for us according to the will of God.

See Romans 8:26–27

V. Come, Holy Spirit. Fill the hearts of your faithful.
R. And kindle in them the fire of your love.
V. Send forth your spirit and they shall be created.
R. And you shall renew the face of the earth.

Let us pray.
O God, you instructed the hearts of the faithful by the light of the Holy Spirit; grant us in the same Spirit to be truly wise, and ever to rejoice in his consolation.
Through Christ our Lord. Amen.

Offering of Oneself to the Holy Spirit

Divine Holy Spirit, love of the Father and of the Son,
through the hands of Mary, your most pure spouse,
and upon the altar of the heart of Jesus,
I offer you myself today and every day of my life.
I offer you my daily labors, my every action, my every breath,
with all my love and every beat of my heart.
Grant that today and every day I may heed
your inspiration and, in all things,
accomplish your will. Amen.

May the Sacred

Prayer to the Holy Spirit, the Secret of Sanctity

I am going to reveal to you the secret of sanctity and happiness. Every day for five minutes control your imagination and close your eyes to all the noises of the world in order to enter into yourself. Then, in the sanctuary of your baptized soul, which is the temple of the Holy Spirit, speak to that Divine Spirit, saying to him:

O Holy Spirit, beloved of my soul,
I adore you.
Enlighten me. Guide me.
Strengthen me. Console me.
Tell me what I should do—direct me.
I promise to submit myself to all that you ask of me,
and I accept all that you permit to happen to me.
Let me only know your will.

If you do this, your life will flow along happily, serenely, and full of consolation, even in the midst of trials. Grace will be proportioned to the trial, giving you the strength to carry it even until you arrive at the gate of paradise, laden with merit. This submission to the Holy Spirit is the secret of sanctity.

Désiré-Joseph Cardinal Mercier

Prayer for Holiness of Life

Breathe in me, O Holy Spirit,
that my thoughts may all be holy.
Act in me, O Holy Spirit,
that my work, too, may be holy.
Draw my heart, O Holy Spirit,
that I may love only what is holy.
Strengthen me, O Holy Spirit,
that I may defend all that is holy.
Guard me, O Holy Spirit,
that I may always be holy.

Saint Augustine

An Act of Love

O my God, I love you above all things, with my whole heart
and soul, because you are all-good and worthy of all love.
I love my neighbor as myself for the love of you. I forgive all
who have injured me, and I ask pardon of all whom I have

Divine Praises in Honor of the Holy Spirit

Glory to the Holy Spirit forever.

Glory to the Comforter forever.

Glory to the Spirit of truth forever.

Glory to the Spirit of grace and prayer forever.

Glory to the Spirit of Jesus forever.

Glory to the Spirit of the Father and the Son forever.

Glory to the Third Person of the adorable Trinity forever.

Blessed James Alberione

To Obtain the Gifts of the Holy Spirit

Come, Holy Spirit, Spirit of Wisdom! Teach us to discern and love the wisdom of the Lord. Your fire tests all wisdom of this world. Your wind overturns the mighty and raises up the lowly.

Come, Holy Spirit, Spirit of Understanding! You alone know the mind of God. Only in you can we fathom the mysteries of divine Revelation; only through you do we recognize the path we are called to follow. Enlighten our minds.

Come, Holy Spirit, Spirit of Counsel! You banish doubt and uncertainty. Through you is the will of God revealed to us. Help and guide us in living this will.

Come, Holy Spirit, Spirit of Fortitude! Uphold us when we are weak. In your strength the apostles, martyrs, and confessors found the courage to witness to Christ with their very lives.

Come, Holy Spirit, Spirit of Knowledge! In creation we recognize your might; in revelation, your wisdom; in our redemption, your love. Teach us to see everything in relation to God.

Come, Holy Spirit, Spirit of Piety! Enkindle in us divine love. In you we have received the spirit of adoption as sons and daughters so that, full of joy, we dare to cry: Abba, loving Father!

Mary Leonora Wilson, FSP

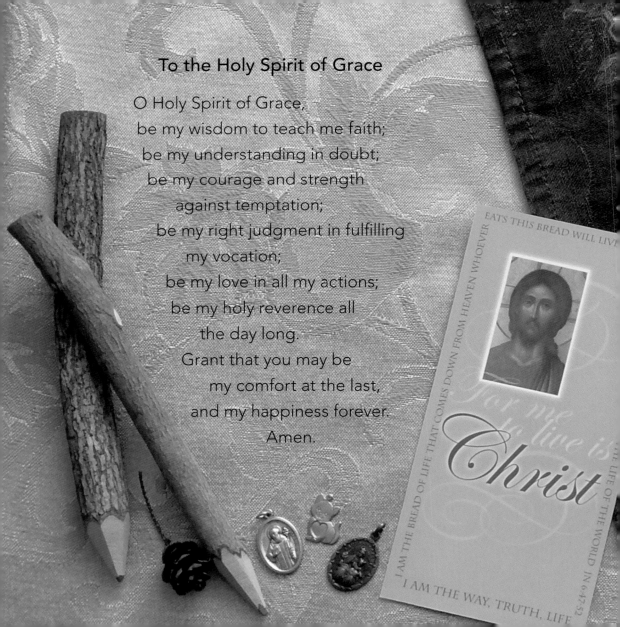

To the Holy Spirit of Grace

O Holy Spirit of Grace,
be my wisdom to teach me faith;
be my understanding in doubt;
be my courage and strength
against temptation;
be my right judgment in fulfilling
my vocation;
be my love in all my actions;
be my holy reverence all
the day long.
Grant that you may be
my comfort at the last,
and my happiness forever.
Amen.

EATS THIS BREAD WILL LIVE

For me to live is
Christ

I AM THE WAY, TRUTH, LIFE

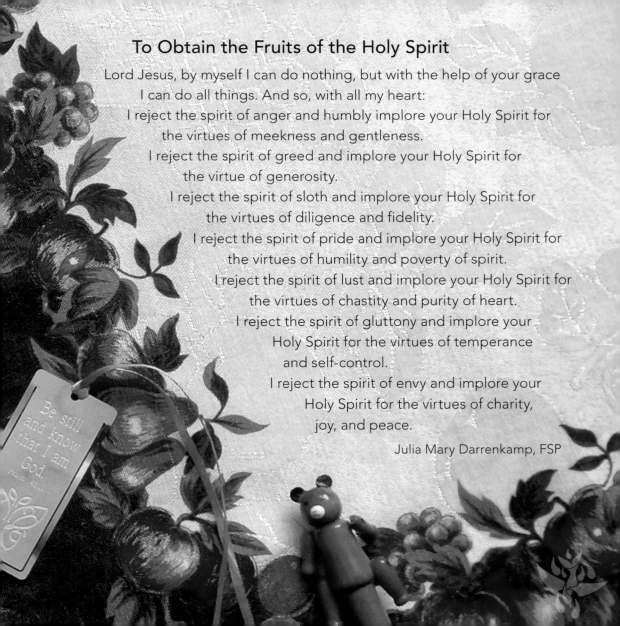

To Obtain the Fruits of the Holy Spirit

Lord Jesus, by myself I can do nothing, but with the help of your grace
I can do all things. And so, with all my heart:
I reject the spirit of anger and humbly implore your Holy Spirit for
the virtues of meekness and gentleness.
I reject the spirit of greed and implore your Holy Spirit for
the virtue of generosity.
I reject the spirit of sloth and implore your Holy Spirit for
the virtues of diligence and fidelity.
I reject the spirit of pride and implore your Holy Spirit for
the virtues of humility and poverty of spirit.
I reject the spirit of lust and implore your Holy Spirit for
the virtues of chastity and purity of heart.
I reject the spirit of gluttony and implore your
Holy Spirit for the virtues of temperance
and self-control.
I reject the spirit of envy and implore your
Holy Spirit for the virtues of charity,
joy, and peace.

Julia Mary Darrenkamp, FSP

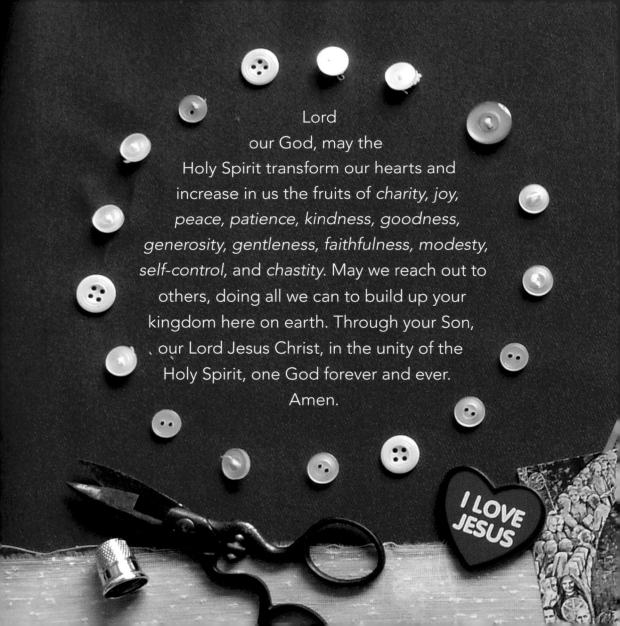

Lord
our God, may the
Holy Spirit transform our hearts and
increase in us the fruits of *charity, joy,*
peace, patience, kindness, goodness,
generosity, gentleness, faithfulness, modesty,
self-control, and *chastity.* May we reach out to
others, doing all we can to build up your
kingdom here on earth. Through your Son,
our Lord Jesus Christ, in the unity of the
Holy Spirit, one God forever and ever.
Amen.

I LOVE JESUS

For Purity of Heart

O Holy Spirit,
living water and radiant fire,
cleanse my heart with the outpouring
of your grace
and fill it with the fire of your love.
Holy Spirit, God of Love,
dwell forever in my heart.

For Discernment

Almighty God, we ask you to send
your Holy Spirit into our hearts
that we may be directed according to your will.
Defend us from error, and guide us to all truth
so that steadfast in faith, we may increase in love
and in all good works.
We ask this through your son
Jesus Christ, our Lord. Amen.

For One's Family and Friends

Holy Spirit, Love of the Father and the Son,
hear my prayer for all those
whom you have given me to love.
By the love you have for them I pray you—
protect them from all harm,
deliver them from evil,
comfort them in sorrow,
reassure them in anxiety,
give them your own joy,
and draw them to yourself.

Brian Moore, SJ

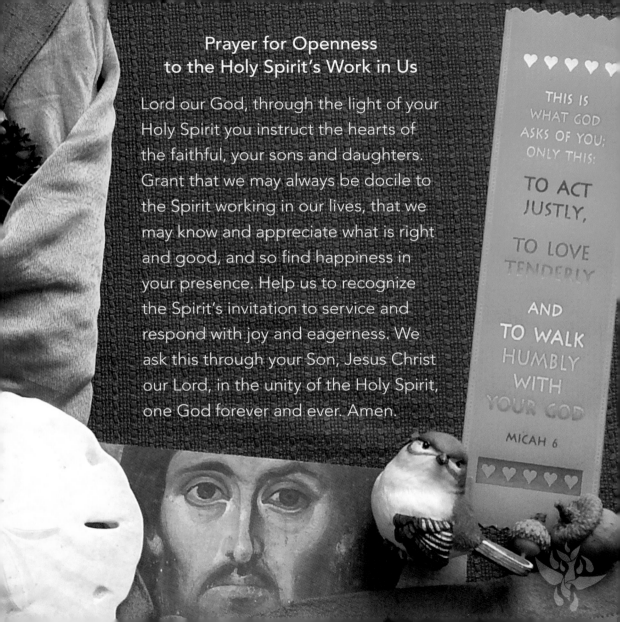

Prayer for Openness to the Holy Spirit's Work in Us

Lord our God, through the light of your Holy Spirit you instruct the hearts of the faithful, your sons and daughters. Grant that we may always be docile to the Spirit working in our lives, that we may know and appreciate what is right and good, and so find happiness in your presence. Help us to recognize the Spirit's invitation to service and respond with joy and eagerness. We ask this through your Son, Jesus Christ our Lord, in the unity of the Holy Spirit, one God forever and ever. Amen.

THIS IS WHAT GOD ASKS OF YOU; ONLY THIS:

TO ACT JUSTLY,

TO LOVE TENDERLY

AND TO WALK HUMBLY WITH YOUR GOD

MICAH 6

Lectio Divina

How to Pray with Scripture

A very ancient way of praying with the Bible is called "Holy Reading," or Lectio Divina. It has five simple steps.

Step One: Lectio (Reading)

Choose a passage of Scripture. It can be long or short, about something relevant to your life, or selected at random. There are some suggestions in the next section of this book. Before reading, ask the Holy Spirit to speak to you through the Scripture you are about to read. Then, read the passage you have selected slowly, perhaps more than once. Take notice of any word, phrase, or image that catches your attention.

Step Two: Meditatio (Meditation)

The second step is to reread the same passage and reflect on what God is saying to you through the word, phrase, or image that attracted you.

Is God challenging you? Asking something of you? Consoling or encouraging you? Reflect on how you can put God's invitation into practice. Resolve to do it throughout the day.

Step Three: Oratio (Verbal Prayer)

In the third step, you may choose to reread the passage again, or not. Having "heard" God speak, it is now your chance to respond. You can use your own words, or words from the Scripture passage you have been praying with. Enter into a conversation with God, asking for help and telling him what is in your heart.

Step Four: Contemplatio (Contemplation)

Remember the word, phrase, or image that touched you. You can silently repeat it throughout the day and carry God's word to you into your life. This will also help you to maintain your resolution to act on God's invitation.

Look Up and Pray.

The Holy Bible

John 3:5–8	Born of the Spirit
Acts 2:1–4	Pentecost
1 Corinthians 12:4–11	Different gifts, but the same spirit
1 Corinthians 2:10–16	No one comprehends God without the Spirit
Romans 8:12–17	You have received a spirit of adoption
John 14:15–25	Coming Advocate
John 16:4–15	The Spirit will guide you into truth
Romans 8:26–27	We do not know how to pray as we ought
Ephesians 1:16–19	Paul's prayer for the Spirit on the faithful
Titus 3:4–7	Saved by rebirth in the Spirit
Ephesians 1:3–14	Spirit of wisdom for faith
Romans 5:3–5	God's love poured into hearts through the Holy Spirit
Romans 15:13	Hope from the Holy Spirit
John 20:19–23	"Receive the Holy Spirit . . ."
2 Thessalonians 2:13	You were chosen by God
Luke 10:21–22	Jesus rejoices in the Spirit
Ezekiel 36:25–28	"I will give you a new spirit"
2 Timothy 1:13–14	Guard sound teaching by the Spirit
1 John 2:27–28	His anointing teaches you
Psalm 139:7	Where can I hide from your spirit?

The Catechism of the Catholic Church

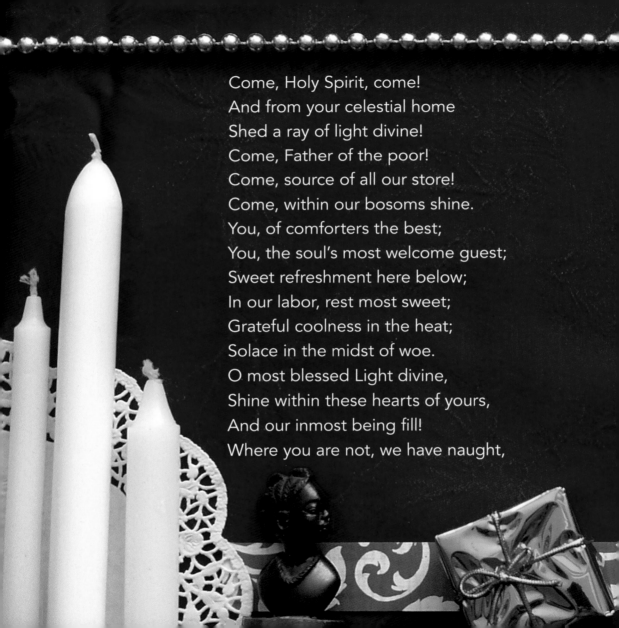

Come, Holy Spirit, come!
And from your celestial home
Shed a ray of light divine!
Come, Father of the poor!
Come, source of all our store!
Come, within our bosoms shine.
You, of comforters the best;
You, the soul's most welcome guest;
Sweet refreshment here below;
In our labor, rest most sweet;
Grateful coolness in the heat;
Solace in the midst of woe.
O most blessed Light divine,
Shine within these hearts of yours,
And our inmost being fill!
Where you are not, we have naught,

Nothing good in deed or thought,
Nothing free from taint of ill.
Heal our wounds, our strength renew;
On our dryness pour your dew;
Wash the stains of guilt away:
Bend the stubborn heart and will;
Melt the frozen, warm the chill;
Guide the steps that go astray.
On the faithful, who adore
And confess you, evermore
In your sevenfold gift descend;
Give them virtue's sure reward;
Give them your salvation, Lord;
Give them joys that never end.

Amen. Alleluia.

Veni, Sancte Spiritus
Gospel Sequence
  for Pentecost

POPE FRANCIS

Biography

Pope Francis is the first pope from the Americas. He was born in Buenos Aires, Argentina on December 17, 1936. His parents named him Jorge Mario Bergoglio. Jorge was like other Argentinean boys. He played and prayed, studied, and got a job when he was a teenager.

One day, seventeen-year-old Jorge stopped by a church to pray on the way to meet his friends. Talking with the priest there, he decided to go to confession. Afterward, Jorge prayed a little longer. Though he had never considered it before, it was clear to Jorge that God was calling him to be a priest. He sought advice and took the time he needed to make such an important decision. Two years later, Jorge Bergoglio entered the seminary.

There were many challenges along the way to Jorge's goal of becoming a priest. While he was still studying at the seminary, Jorge became very ill. One of his lungs became infected, and a large part of it had to be surgically removed. When he was well again, Jorge decided to leave the diocesan seminary he had been attending. Instead, he entered the Society of Jesus and continued his studies at the Jesuit seminary. He was ordained a Jesuit priest in 1969.

From 1973–1979, Father Jorge Bergoglio was the Provincial Superior of the Jesuit community in Argentina. These were difficult years because of the political turmoil in the country. In 1992, he was selected to be an auxiliary bishop in Buenos Aires. This gave him more opportunity to serve the poor, to preach the Good News, and teach young people—all aspects of the priesthood that he loved.

He would have been happy in this role forever; however, in 1998, Pope John Paul II chose Bishop Jorge to become the new archbishop of Buenos Aires. As archbishop, he insisted on living a very simple life. He chose to live in a small apartment instead of the large archbishop's residence. Archbishop Jorge also continued to use public transportation and talked with the people wherever he was.

Three years later, the archbishop was named a cardinal. When Pope John Paul II died in 2005, he found himself traveling to Rome to elect the next pope. The College of Cardinals chose Joseph Ratzinger, who became Pope Benedict XVI. Benedict XVI served as pope for eight years. Then he unexpectedly announced that he had decided to retire. Cardinal Jorge again went to Rome in 2013 for a papal election. This time the cardinals chose him. Both he and the rest of the world were surprised because there had never been a Jesuit pope or a Latin American pope. As Pope Francis, he continues his simple style of living and is always ready to offer a smile along with a word of encouragement for those who follow Christ.

notes

mine

mentors

thoughts

yours

family

prayers

friends

messages

HANDLE WITH CARE

Credits
In order of appearance

Page 8—*L'Osservatore Romano*

Wisdom—iStock.com/VSanandhakrishna; FreeImages.com/Amir Rochman; FreeImages.com/Rudy Tiben; Unsplash.com/Muhammed Fayiz; FreeImages.com/Ryan Aréstegui; FreeImages.com/A. Carlos Herrera; FreeImages.com/Patrick Nijhuis

Understanding—©Faizan Khan | Dreamstime.com; iStock.com/Andreas Arnold; FreeImages.com/Tori Campbell; iStock.com/-art-siberia-; iStock.com/knape; iStock.com/Ken Vander Putten

Counsel—iStock.com/olesiabilkei; iStock.com/Silvia Bianchini; iStock.com/naphtalina; iStock.com/Enrico Fianchini; iStock.com/Aldo Murillo; FreeImages.com/Mario Alberto Magallanes Trejo

Fortitude—Mary Emmanuel Alves, FSP; iStock.com/altanaka; iStock.com/Andrey Shadrin; iStock.com/rusm; iStock.com/kzenon, iStock.com/3Trinity, iStock.com/Witthaya; iStock.com/franckreporter; iStock.com/karelnoppe; iStock.com/Jane1e; iStock.com/PeopleImages

Knowledge—iStock.com/Rawpixel; iStock.com/Paolo Cipriani; iStock.com/ArtMarie; FreeImages.com/Wojciech Bekiesz; Unsplash.com/Patrick Tomasso; Mary Emmanuel Alves, FSP; FreeImages.com/cop richard

Piety— Mary Joseph Peterson, FSP; iStock.com/juanestey; iStock.com/wundervisuals; iStock.com/ThomasVogel; iStock.com/IPGGutenbergUKLtd; ©Tracy Whiteside | Dreamstime.com; iStock.com/Vikram Raghuvanshi; iStock.com/monkeybusinessimages; ©Dmitriy Shironosov | Dreamstime.com; iStock.com/AkilinaWinner; Margaret Joseph Obravac, FSP; iStock.com/Peter Brutsch; iStock.com/monkeybusinessimages; iStock.com/wundervisuals; iStock.com/ferlistockphoto

Fear of the Lord— iStock.com/pilipphoto; Mary Joseph Peterson, FSP; FreeImages.com/Javier Ramirez; FreeImages.com/Asif Akbar; Mary Emmanuel Alves, FSP/Laura Rosemarie McGowan, FSP; Mary Emmanuel Alves, FSP

Prayers—Mary Joseph Peterson, FSP

Pope Francis Biography—flaglane.com; L'Osservatore Romano

All
glory,
praise,
and honor
be to
God
our Father
above!

Pauline TEEN

Who: The Daughters of St. Paul

What: Pauline Teen—linking your life to Jesus Christ and his Church

When: 24/7

Where: All over the world and on www.pauline.org

Why: Because our life-long passion is to witness to God's amazing love for all people!

How: Inspiring lives of holiness through: APPS, digital media, concerts, websites, social media, videos, blogs, books, music albums, radio, media literacy, DVDs, ebooks, stores, conferences, bookfairs, parish exhibits, personal contact, illustration, vocation talks, photography, writing, editing, graphic design, marketing, inter

smile
God loves you

Pauline
BOOKS & MEDIA

The Daughters of St. Paul operate book and media centers
at the following addresses. Visit, call, or write the one nearest you today,
or find us at www.paulinestore.org.

CALIFORNIA
3908 Sepulveda Blvd, Culver City, CA 90230   310-397-8676
3250 Middlefield Road, Menlo Park, CA 94025   650-369-4230

FLORIDA
145 SW 107th Avenue, Miami, FL 33174   305-559-6715

HAWAII
1143 Bishop Street, Honolulu, HI 96813   808-521-2731

ILLINOIS
172 North Michigan Avenue, Chicago, IL 60601   312-346-4228

LOUISIANA
4403 Veterans Memorial Blvd, Metairie, LA 70006   504-887-7631

MASSACHUSETTS
885 Providence Hwy, Dedham, MA 02026   781-326-5385

MISSOURI
9804 Watson Road, St. Louis, MO 63126   314-965-3512

NEW YORK
64 West 38th Street, New York, NY 10018   212-754-1110

SOUTH CAROLINA
243 King Street, Charleston, SC 29401   843-577-0175

TEXAS — Currently no book center; for parish exhibits or outreach evangelization,
contact: 210-569-0500 or SanAntonio@paulinemedia.com or P.O. Box 761416,
San Antonio, TX 78245

VIRGINIA
1025 King Street, Alexandria, VA 22314   703-549-3806

CANADA
3022 Dufferin Street, Toronto, ON M6B 3T5   416-781-9131